The Puppet's Eye

Ian Bone
AR B.L.: 3.2
Points: 1.0   MG

THE PUPPET'S EYE

by Ian Bone

illustrated by Shaun Tan

Cover illustration by Richard Pellegrino

Librarian Reviewer
Marci Peschke
Librarian, Dallas Independent School District
MA Education Reading Specialist, Stephen F. Austin State University
Learning Resources Endorsement, Texas Women's University

Reading Consultant
Elizabeth Stedem
Educator/Consultant, Colorado Springs, CO
MA in Elementary Education, University of Denver, CO

STONE ARCH BOOKS
www.stonearchbooks.com

First published in the United States in 2008
by Stone Arch Books
151 Good Counsel Drive, P.O. Box 669
Mankato, Minnesota 56002
www.stonearchbooks.com

Text copyright © 1999 Ian Bone
Illustrations copyright © 1999 Shaun

First published in Australia in 1999 by Lothian Books
(now Hachette Livre Australia Pty Ltd)
under the title *The Puppet*

Published in arrangement with Hachette Livre Australia.

Library of Congress Cataloging-in-Publication Data
Bone, Ian, 1956–
    The Puppet's Eye / by Ian Bone; illustrated by Shaun Tan.
    p. cm. — (Shade Books)
    ISBN 978-1-4342-0793-7 (library binding)
    ISBN 978-1-4342-0889-7 (pbk.)
    [1. Fathers and sons—Fiction. 2. Puppets—Fiction. 3. Horror
stories.] I. Tan, Shaun, ill. II. Title.
PZ7.B63697Pu 2009
[Fic]—dc22   2008008009

Summary: Tim visits the set of the TV show where his father works.
The star of the show is just a puppet, so why does the puppetmaster
treat it like a real boy?

Art Director: Heather Kindseth
Graphic Designer: Kay Fraser

1 2 3 4 5 6 13 12 11 10 09 08

TABLE OF CONTENTS

CHAPTER 1

THE
PHOTOGRAPH

A photograph of the puppet sat on the car's dashboard. It was reflected every now and then in the windshield.

The image of its weird puppet smile mingled with the dusty smears on the windshield, then *flash*!

It vanished in the shadow of some trees as Tim McLachlan and his father, Patrick, drove down the street.

Flash! The image was reflected again in full color as the car burst into sunshine.

Flash . . . gone. *Flash* . . . smile.

Flash . . . gone!

The strange picture was giving Tim the creeps. He placed his jacket over the photograph, covering it up. Then he glanced at his father.

"Why did you do that?" Patrick snapped. "Put your coat somewhere else."

Tim grabbed his jacket. The photograph slid onto his lap.

"Put that back," his father said.

Tim put the photograph back on the dashboard. Then he tried to shrink into as small a space as possible.

The day was off to a bad start.

Tim had been forced to spend the weekend with his father. He hardly knew the man. His father had walked out on Tim and his mother years ago.

Tim only saw him at Christmas and sometimes on his birthday. Usually, Patrick would arrive with an awful present. He'd mumble a few words. Then he'd leave as soon as he could.

But when Tim's mom had to go out of town, she said he had to stay with his father.

"Can't I stay with Jake?" Tim had begged. "His parents won't mind."

"They've got five kids, honey," his mom had said, shaking her head. "They don't need any more. Besides, it'll be a chance for you to hang out with your dad. Plus, he's working at the TV station on Saturday. You'll get to go with him."

So Tim had been forced to go to his dad's.

The only thing that made it okay was that it might be cool to watch a TV show being filmed.

Patrick worked at Channel 8. He was the boss of something called "staging." That meant he built sets and props.

By Saturday morning, when it was time to leave, Tim was actually looking forward to the weekend. But his mother took forever to pack, and they arrived at Patrick's apartment really late.

Patrick was already outside, waiting next to his car.

As Tim started to get out of his mom's car, his mother touched him on the arm. "Remember," she said nervously, "your father can be a difficult man. He's not very good with kids."

Tim nodded and got out. His father was waiting, an angry look in his eyes.

"Sorry," said Tim weakly.

"Get in," grumbled Patrick, climbing into his car. "We're late."

Then they left.

Patrick frowned as he drove. It seemed like it was going to be a really long weekend. But Tim tried to look on the bright side. At least he was going to the TV station. That was cool.

He turned to his dad and asked, "What TV show are you making today?"

Patrick didn't reply. He kept frowning.

Tim looked at him. He remembered sneaking into Patrick's workshop when he was a little boy.

He liked being in the workshop. He wanted to watch his dad working.

"What's this do?" Tim would ask. "Can I help?"

His dad would just say, "Leave me alone."

Once Tim had brought home a wooden boat he'd made at school. He couldn't have been older than six, and the boat was nothing more than a few pieces of wood barely put together. Still, he was proud when he showed it to his father.

Tim's dad had smiled. Then he'd said, "It doesn't look like a boat at all."

He took it out to his workshop and started fixing it. Tim followed him and watched from a corner.

Tim stared out the window at the passing cars. He remembered feeling stupid and weak as his father straightened each crooked edge and replaced the bad nails.

"*Dr. Riddle*," said Patrick. "That's the show we're taping today."

"Oh," Tim said. He tried not to sound too disappointed.

Dr. Riddle was the puppet in the photograph on the dashboard. He was the star of a boring kids show. The puppet asked riddles that anyone could answer. It was not the kind of show that Tim watched.

Tim had been hoping to get to see something more interesting, like a show with famous actors.

"Are you working on any other shows today?" asked Tim.

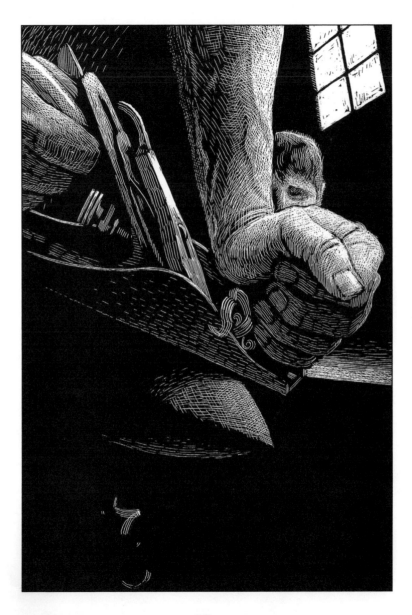

Patrick didn't answer. Instead, he drummed the steering wheel in an angry way, as if there was something bothering him. Finally he yelled, "Shows like *Dr. Riddle* are my work. That's what I do. Do you understand that?"

"Sure," replied Tim. He paused. "Do you ever get to meet famous people?" he asked.

Patrick laughed meanly and shook his head. "TV's not like they say it is in the magazines," he told Tim.

"I know that," Tim muttered. He hated it when his father made him feel stupid.

"The famous people," Patrick went on, "are only a small part of what goes on. It's the workers, working hard, who make TV shows happen. I stick by them, they stick by me." His voice was louder now.

Tim glanced at the photo of the puppet. It had a little wooden head with a fake, painted-on smile. That was his father's work.

"Remember that, okay? It's called loyalty," said Patrick. Then he sighed, and went back to his old silent self. His cold eyes stared at the road.

Loyalty. Tim wanted to laugh. He used to believe in loyalty, when he was little, when he thought his dad would come back. Now he knew better.

Loyalty was a joke. And the only one smiling was the puppet.

CHAPTER 2

DR.
RIDDLE

As they walked in through the huge studio doors at Channel 8, Tim whispered, "Wow!" He was dazzled by all of the lights hanging from the ceiling.

There were people running everywhere, shouting. Someone yelled, "Patrick, come and take a look at this!"

"Stay where you are," Tim's father told him. Then Tim was left alone in the middle of the craziness. He stood and looked around the crowded room.

Two women pushed TV cameras toward the brightly lit *Dr. Riddle* set. "Watch out!" one of them called.

Tim stepped sideways to avoid crashing into them. But then he was almost run over by a man pushing a cart. The man shouted, "Careful!"

Someone laughed loudly behind Tim. He turned around, but whoever it was passed by quickly.

A loud banging above his head startled him. He looked up and saw a man dangling from the ceiling near the lights, changing a bulb.

Everyone was busy. Everyone had a job to do. Tim wondered if he should move out of the way.

Then a woman with a clipboard walked over to him. "Who are you?" she asked.

"Um, I'm Tim," Tim said nervously.

"He's mine," called Patrick, running across the studio.

"Oh, okay, Patrick," the woman said. "You should have let me know."

"Sorry," Patrick said. "His visit was a last-minute surprise." He grabbed Tim's arm. His grip hurt.

Patrick led Tim to a dark corner, where some chairs were set up. "Sit here," he said. Then he walked away.

Tim watched from his lonely spot in the corner as his father worked. Everyone went to Patrick with their problems.

"Patrick, can you fix this?" they would yell.

Or they'd say, "Patrick, do you have a minute?"

Tim's father answered every question, tended to every need. His hands looked so strong and careful. They knew what to do. They could fix anything.

Tim wondered what it would be like if those hands patted him on the back. He looked down, suddenly sad.

A shadow fell in front of Tim. He looked up. A young man wearing overalls was standing in front of him. "They call him Mr. Fixit," the guy said.

"Huh?" said Tim.

"Patrick," the guy said, smiling and pointing at Tim's father. "My name's Chris." He sat down on the edge of a chair.

"Hi. Um, it's okay for me to be here," said Tim. "I'm with Patrick."

"Relax," Chris said. "I know already. I'm his assistant. He's a secretive guy, your dad. I never knew he had a son."

"Oh," Tim said. He felt slightly shocked. Talking was never one of his father's strong points, but Tim thought his dad would have mentioned having a son.

"Yep," Chris went on. "I always thought Patrick wasn't the dad type. So, are you like your dad? A younger Mr. Fixit?"

Tim blushed. "Not really," he mumbled. He looked over and saw Patrick talking to an old man. Their heads were almost touching. It was strange. Tim had never seen his father stand so close to anyone before.

"This place couldn't work without your dad," said Chris.

Tim nodded. He looked over at the old man again. Who was he? Who was the special person who could talk to his father for so long?

The old man looked up and turned toward Tim. Could the man see him, tucked away in the dark corner? Had Patrick told the man to look? Was he saying, "That's my kid — he's always in the way."

Whatever it was, the old man shook his head quickly and walked away. He seemed angry about something.

"Hey," said Chris. "I have to go down to the prop room. Want to come with me?"

Tim hesitated. Was he allowed to move from his dark little corner?

"Come on. It's where all the ghosts of TV hang out," Chris added, smiling.

Chris stood up and headed out of the studio, pushing a cart in front of him.

Tim paused for a moment. Then he followed Chris. What harm could it do?

CHAPTER 3

THE PROP
ROOM

The prop room was lined with huge shelves. The shelves were loaded with every object you could think of.

One row was packed with telephones. Another row of shelves was full of fake weapons.

"What do you think?" asked Chris, as he pushed his cart between the rows.

"Awesome," said Tim.

"Too big, if you ask me," Chris muttered.

"You could get lost in this place," said Tim. He couldn't help thinking how much fun it would be to get his hands on some of the stuff.

Chris reached up and pulled down a vase of plastic flowers. "Your dad loves this puppet show," he told Tim. "Don't ask me why. Have you met the puppet master yet? He's a creep. You should hear what he calls that puppet. 'Our little boy.' Seriously. But only to Patrick. Weird, huh?"

Tim nodded, but he wasn't really paying attention. He picked up a real-looking dagger from a shelf and ran his finger over the edge.

"Hey, did you know they found a body in here once?" said Chris, grinning.

That got Tim's attention. "No way," he said.

"It's true," Chris said. "The body of a guy named Codey. He was the head of staging, before your dad."

Chris pretended to move a knife across his throat.

"Dead. Right where you're standing," he said, pointing at the ground where Tim stood.

Tim stepped back. Then he blushed when Chris laughed. He could see that Chris was making fun of him.

"Was he really murdered?" Tim asked.

"Nah," Chris said. "Well, maybe, but not here. Old man Codey just vanished off the face of the earth. No one knows what happened to him."

Chris pulled a list from his pocket, looked at it, and then shook his head. He said, "I'm way behind today. Hey! You can help. Go to row Q and see if you can find an alarm clock. A big one, okay?"

"Sure," said Tim. It was a relief to be able to do something instead of just sitting and watching.

He found row Q, but he didn't see any alarm clocks. One shelf had a black curtain hanging over it. Tim pulled it aside, hoping to find the clocks.

A disgusting face, full of sadness and pain, flew out of the darkness at him.

Tim screamed and jumped back.

Then he felt stupid. It was only a rubber mask. He hoped Chris hadn't heard him scream.

There were about twenty masks on the shelf, each more disgusting than the last. Tim picked one up. It looked so real — the hair, the eyes, even the skin. He shuddered. What kind of TV show needed that?

A cold breeze blew across Tim's face, and he turned around. Had someone opened a door? There was nothing but shelves behind him.

He looked up and saw an open window. Two pigeons flew in, their flapping wings making a racket.

Tim smiled. That's where the wind had come from.

He started to put the mask back. But then he heard a sound, a laugh somewhere far away. He dropped the mask and froze. Had he imagined it?

He listened. There it was again. It was very quiet.

"Hello?" he called.

No reply.

"Chris?" he said.

Silence.

Someone was watching him, he was sure of it. Was it Chris, playing a joke?

"Hey, Chris, I can't find a clock," Tim yelled.

Nothing.

There was a crawling feeling on the back of his neck. He spun around, expecting to see someone standing there.

"Is someone there?" Tim yelled.

Nothing.

Tim turned and ran.

CHAPTER 4

THE PUPPET MASTER

Halfway down a long, dark hallway, Tim stopped and caught his breath. He was lost. He wished he'd paid more attention when Chris had led him to the prop room.

This part of the building was like a maze. He had no idea which way the studio was. Taking a guess, he walked down one hallway and saw a door closing. It had to be Chris.

"Chris?" Tim called.

Tim reached for the door handle, but before he could turn it, a strange noise stopped him. It was a high-pitched little boy's voice.

That meant it wasn't Chris behind the door, but it might be someone who knew the way back to the studio.

Tim opened the door just a crack. He could see an empty room. The only thing in it was a large chair, right in the middle of the room.

The old man who had been talking to Tim's father sat in the chair. He was holding the puppet, with its bright, painted eyes and weird grin.

That's when Tim realized that the old man was the puppet master. He couldn't see Tim, hidden behind the door.

"What is lighter than a feather," said the puppet master in the weird, high voice, "but can knock down a tree?"

Wind, thought Tim. That was easy.

Tim almost answered the riddle out loud, but another voice spoke first.

"I'm worried," the puppet said. His voice was identical to the old man's. "He brought a stranger into our house."

"A stranger," the old man echoed.

Tim shook his head. Listening to them talk was weird. The two voices were exactly the same. The only real clue about who was speaking was the slight movement of lips, and even they didn't quite match up. Tim watched carefully.

"We can't let him get away with it," one of them said. Who was talking, the puppet or the puppet master? Tim couldn't tell.

"He must pay. It's what we ask for." Tim still couldn't tell who said it.

What are they talking about? Tim wondered. *Who has to pay*?

Tim let go of the door handle. It made a sharp click.

Both faces spun around to look at him. Anger burned in the old man's eyes, but it was the eyes of the puppet that nailed Tim to the spot.

They seemed alive. They seemed to stare right through Tim.

"Sorry," muttered Tim.

The puppet turned to its master. "He's come to hurt me! He's come to hurt me!" the puppet screamed.

Tim stumbled backward. His eyes were locked on the little wooden face, on those little wooden eyes.

The eyes burned him with their coldness. The painted mouth seemed to turn down at the corners, almost like it was angry.

Tim turned and ran down the hall. Then he ran right into Chris.

"Where have you been?" Chris asked.

Tim stopped, catching his breath.

"Did you find a clock?" asked Chris.

Tim shook his head.

Chris sighed. "Your dad's going to kill me. We're really late," he said.

He gave Tim directions back to the studio. Then Chris hurried off to the prop room.

Tim felt bad about letting Chris down. He closed his eyes and leaned against the wall.

Inside his head, the little wooden smile chased him, laughing at him.

Tim shook his head. Then he made his way back to the studio. He felt like he was being watched and laughed at. Everyone laughed at the useless kid who messed everything up.

CHAPTER 5

HE'S DEAD!

Patrick was furious.

"Where's Chris?" he demanded as soon as Tim walked into the studio.

"He's in the prop room," Tim said. He hated that his father made him feel so bad. He wanted to sit for five minutes and try to calm down. But Patrick stood there, red-faced and frowning.

"Come with me," Tim's father said finally. His voice was angry. "I'll have to use you to help."

"Me?" asked Tim nervously.

Patrick sighed. "Yes," he said. "Come on."

He led Tim over to the set and said, "Hold this up for me."

Patrick pointed at a big piece of wood. It was part of a piece of scenery. It looked like part of a wall. Tim nodded. That seemed easy enough.

Patrick went around to the other side. Tim stretched his arms wide, holding onto the edges of the piece of scenery. It was tall and heavy. Tim had to lean against it to support the weight.

"You got it?" called Patrick.

"Yes," Tim called back.

He heard drilling as Patrick fixed whatever was broken. Tim hoped his father wasn't going to take too long. The piece of wood was growing heavier by the second.

"Hold it steady," Patrick yelled.

Tim gripped the piece of scenery tighter, but his arms were beginning to shake. He didn't know how much longer he could hold it up.

"Dad . . ." he whispered.

"Hold still!" Patrick ordered.

Tim's arms started shaking. His face turned red and he started to feel stupid. He was Mr. Fixit's son, and he couldn't even do a simple job like hold on to a piece of scenery.

He knew that everyone was watching him, thinking, "That kid is useless. He's nothing like his dad."

Tim started to feel dizzy. Everything began to swirl around him.

Then an evil, angry voice whispered in his ear, "We don't want you."

"What?" said Tim. He looked up and saw the wrinkled face of the puppet master.

The puppet master was holding the puppet away from Tim, like he was trying to protect it. "He doesn't want you either," the puppet master cried.

"No," said Tim, struggling with the piece of scenery. "No, I'm not, I'm just . . ."

"No one wants you!" the old man yelled. He swung the puppet around and its little hand slapped Tim in the face.

Tim tried to ignore the crazy old man and focus on holding up the piece of scenery. But it was just too heavy. His arms finally gave out.

"Look out!" screamed Tim.

The heavy piece of painted wood jerked wildly to one side. Then it smashed down on Tim and the puppet master.

Tim hit the ground. A sharp pain tore at his arm. Then he saw the puppet hit the floor.

Its wooden head smacked the ground hard, making a sharp, loud crack. It was the worst sound Tim had ever heard.

The studio went crazy. Some people yelled orders. Others ran to help the puppet master. Tim slowly staggered to his feet. His arm was bleeding.

Several people were trying to help the limping puppet master walk to a chair, but he shook them off. The puppet master hurried over to Patrick, who was gently holding the broken puppet.

A large crack ran through one of the puppet's eyes. It was a black, gaping split from forehead to cheek.

"He's dead," whispered the old man. Then he pointed to Tim and yelled, "Murderer!"

Everyone turned to look at Tim, who clutched the painful cut on his arm. He looked at his father. It was an accident. Anyone could see that!

"Get out," Patrick whispered. Then he yelled, "Now!"

Tim stumbled, blinking back tears.

"We'd better go," said a familiar voice. It was Chris. Tim nodded.

He'd ruined everything.

CHAPTER 6

DR. RIDDLE'S EYES

Chris led Tim to the workshop. It was a big, cold room filled with huge metal machines.

"Does it hurt?" Chris asked as he wrapped bandages around Tim's arm.

"No," mumbled Tim.

"Don't worry," Chris said kindly. "Patrick will get you to a doctor."

Tim wasn't even thinking about his arm. He quietly asked, "Will he be able to fix the puppet?"

"Of course," said Chris. "Patrick can fix anything." But he didn't sound very sure.

"That old guy," Tim said. "He said I murdered it."

"Don't worry," Chris said. "The old man's crazy."

Tim shook his head. The old man might be crazy, but he was also right. The puppet did look dead. Earlier, in that strange room, its eyes had been alive. But now, all Tim could see was that terrible crack down the puppet's face.

Chris sat down on a bench, jiggling his legs nervously. "I wonder what we'll do now," he said. "We can't tape the show without the puppet. Man, I bet they're running around like crazy back in the studio. No one touches that puppet. No one. And you wrecked it in one hit. That was really something."

Chris tried to laugh, to lighten the mood, but that only made Tim feel worse.

"I didn't mean to," said Tim.

"No, of course not," said Chris. His legs started jiggling faster and faster. "No one said you did. You need to relax, man."

"I wish I'd never come here," Tim said sadly. "Things were bad enough. Now Dad will think I'm an idiot. Today has been the worst day ever. He'll wish he never brought me here."

"Oh, come on," said Chris. "You're a kid. Kids make mistakes. He's probably mad, but he'll get over it."

Tim shook his head. He'd seen the look on Patrick's face. His father wasn't going to get over it anytime soon.

"Anyway, it's not like you're the only one who's ever damaged that puppet," Chris went on. "I heard Codey cut its hand off by mistake once. The puppet master tried to have him fired, but Codey hung around, until . . ." He paused.

"Until he was murdered," whispered Tim.

The workshop door swung open, and Patrick walked in, holding the puppet.

"Can you can fix it?" asked Chris.

Patrick didn't answer. He took a tool from the wall and a bottle of glue from a cupboard. Then he laid the puppet on the bench.

"I'll be in the studio if you need me," said Chris. Then he took off.

Tim watched his father fill the crack in the puppet's face with glue. He carefully wiped the extra glue away.

It was almost loving, the way he lightly touched the puppet's head with the soft cloth. But Tim could see the anger in his father's face.

Patrick placed the puppet's head in a clamp. He turned the handle tighter and tighter. The crack oozed glue, like sticky blood, and Patrick rubbed it away.

"Will it be all right?" asked Tim, when the silence became unbearable.

"No," his father replied. "Dr. Riddle will never be the same again."

Tim wanted to ask why his father couldn't fix the puppet. But he didn't.

Patrick took a sheet of sandpaper from a drawer and began rubbing the puppet's cracked eye. More paint came off with every stroke. The puppet's little head jerked back and forth, and Tim nearly screamed. Those eyes had been alive only half an hour ago. They had been laughing at him.

"Stop," said Tim. He didn't want to watch anymore. He felt so guilty.

His father continued sanding. It seemed like he wanted Tim to see how much damage he had done.

"Stop," Tim said, louder.

Patrick kept sanding. "Dad!" Tim yelled.

Sweat dripped from Patrick's face. He looked at his son. Then he laid the sandpaper down.

Tim's father reached for a can of paint and pulled a small brush out of his pocket. Then he began to touch up the puppet's eye. His hand was so quick, so careful and gentle.

Suddenly, Tim realized something. "You made the puppet," he said. His father nodded. "I never knew," Tim said quietly.

Patrick dried the paint with a hairdryer. Then he began to add the colorful details of the eye.

Tim was amazed at his father's work. The two eyes were almost the same now. It seemed like there was a chance that the puppet would be as good as new.

But when Tim looked closely at the finished job, there was still something missing. The life was gone.

Tim slumped back in his chair. His moment of hope was over. He had wrecked everything.

The wooden eyes of Dr. Riddle would never be the same.

CHAPTER 7

BLOOD FOR BLOOD

A group of people came into the workshop to look at Patrick's work on the puppet.

They talked in hushed, worried tones. No one dared to look over at Tim, sitting sadly in a corner.

Some of the people wanted to keep going with the day's taping. Others wanted to cancel it. Soon, everyone was fighting about what they should do next. One thing was clear. Everyone was upset.

Patrick suggested they take a lunch break and think it over. Everyone agreed, and the group left.

When everyone was gone, Tim realized that the puppet master was sitting quietly in the other corner of the room.

"He's gone," the old man said, shaking his bandaged head. "I can't feel him anymore."

"Take a closer look," said Patrick. "The life will come back. You're just not used to this new paint job."

"No!" shouted the puppet master. "Our little boy is dead. You know that. Don't treat me like an idiot."

He shuffled over to the workbench and picked up the puppet's body. Then he held the tiny face up to his nose and sniffed.

What was he trying to smell? The paint job? The puppet's breath?

Tim looked at his father for a clue, but Patrick's face was blank. If he thought the puppet master's behavior was strange, Patrick wasn't showing it.

"There is a chance," said the old man. Tim leaned forward. "There just might be a way to get the life back."

"What do you have in mind?" asked Patrick.

The old man chuckled. "Oh, I think you know what I'm talking about," he said. Then he turned to Tim and looked him up and down.

"Funny, isn't it?" the old man went on. "The puppet was made by the father and destroyed by the son!"

"I'm sorry," Tim whispered. "I didn't mean to."

The puppet master held up his hand for silence. "There is only one way," he said. "A soul for a soul. Blood for blood. It was done before. It can be done again."

Tim looked at his father. "What does he mean?" Tim asked.

Patrick didn't answer. He was staring at the puppet master.

"It was done before," whispered the old man.

"But not by me," said Patrick.

Tim didn't know what they meant. What was done before? It sounded like something bad.

Then his blood froze.

Had they given Codey's life to the puppet?

Tim wrapped his arms around his chest. "What's going on?" he asked in a weak voice.

The puppet master pulled a long knife from his pocket and opened the blade. He held its pearl handle toward Patrick.

"For our little boy," the puppet master whispered.

Patrick took the knife and turned it over in his hands, looking closely at it.

"Please, Dad, stop this," said Tim, pushing back against his chair. "I don't like this!"

"The choice is simple," the puppet master growled.

Tim looked at his father's hand, holding the knife.

Tim tried to speak, but his voice would not come. He was nothing. He was just an annoying kid. He was a useless joke of a son, who couldn't even do a simple job without messing it up.

"Now," whispered the old man. "Do it now!"

Tim's hands gripped the bottom of his T-shirt. He closed his eyes. Then he opened them. Sweat dripped down the sides of his face.

Patrick loosened his grip on the knife. It fell to the floor.

"No," growled the puppet master. He ran to pick up the knife. Then he held it high in the air.

"So much for loyalty, Patrick," he sneered. "I'll do it. For our little boy."

Tim looked at his father. Couldn't he stop this crazy old man? But Patrick seemed unable to move.

Tim's father was frozen, cold. Just like all those years after he'd walked out on his family. He was so far away, so unknown, so untouchable.

The memory made Tim move. He grabbed Patrick by the wrist. "I'm your son!" he yelled.

The puppet master raised the knife.

"Wait!" yelled Patrick, shaking Tim's hand free.

"Yes!" the puppet master cried happily. He handed Patrick the knife. "A son for a son!"

"Dad, please!" begged Tim.

Patrick looked at his son quickly. Tim thought he saw his father's eyes sparkle, as if the man had winked at him. Tim held his breath.

Then Patrick brought the knife down. A rush of air blew across Tim's face. He heard an awful scream that shook his very core.

He couldn't think, he couldn't feel. All he could do was curl into a ball on his chair and sob.

CHAPTER 8

LITTLE BOY

Two rough hands grabbed Tim's shoulders. Tim leaned into their strength.

"Come on, son," said Patrick quietly. "It's all okay now."

Tim stood on shaky legs. Patrick led him from the workshop. On the floor, sobbing like a baby, lay the puppet master. The "boy" was in his arms. The blade of the knife was stuck in its newly painted eye.

ABOUT THE AUTHOR

Ian Bone has written all kinds of books, from picture books to young adult novels. He has been a full-time writer for over twelve years and divides his time between writing his books, designing and writing online educational simulations for universities, teaching creative writing, and making videos. He lives in Australia.

ABOUT THE ILLUSTRATOR

Shaun Tan was born in 1974 and grew up in Australia. As a teenager, Shaun began drawing and painting images for science fiction and horror stories in small press magazines. Since then, he has received numerous awards for his picture books. He has recently worked for Blue Sky Studios and Pixar, providing concept artwork for forthcoming films. His book *The Arrival* was one of the best-reviewed books of 2007.

GLOSSARY

difficult (DIF-uh-kuhlt)—not easy to get along with

loyalty (LOI-uhl-tee)—a firm support or faith in friends or one's job

prop (PROP)—an item that an actor needs to carry or use

riddle (RID-uhl)—a question that seems to make no sense, but that has a clever answer

scenery (SEE-nur-ee)—the painted boards and screens that are used on stage as a background

secretive (SEE-kri-tiv)—tending to be silent and not tell people much about oneself

station (STAY-shuhn)—a place with equipment to send out television or radio signals

studio (STOO-dee-oh)—a place where television shows are made

vanished (VAN-ishd)—disappeared

workshop (WURK-shop)—a room or building where things are made or fixed

DISCUSSION QUESTIONS

1. Why does Tim think that his father doesn't like him?

2. Why does the puppet master get so upset when the puppet is damaged?

3. This book's title is *The Puppet's Eye*. Why do you think this book has that title?

WRITING PROMPTS

1. At the end of this book, Tim and Patrick are both safe. What do you think happens next? Write a page that starts where this story ends.

2. If you worked on a television show, what show would it be? What would you do at your job? Write about it.

3. At the beginning of this book, Tim thinks that his father doesn't like him, but by the end, it is clear that Patrick does care about his son. Have you ever thought that someone disliked you but found out that wasn't true? Write about what happened.

MORE SHADE BOOKS!
Take a deep breath and

THE CURSE OF RAVEN LAKE

BY CHRIS KREIE

CHRIS KREIE
THE CURSE OF RAVEN LAKE

STONE ARCH *Fantasy*

Charlie has wanted to stay alone at his family's cabin for as long as he can remember. When he finally does, the day starts off perfectly. But then the old man next door mentions a curse. When darkness falls, something unseen scratches at the door . . .

Step into the shade!

THE
GHOST
OF J. STOKELY

BOB TEMPLE

THE GHOST OF J. STOKELY

BY BOB TEMPLE

STONE ARCH *Fantasy*

Jared and his friends thought they were going on a fun camping trip at Eagle Point. But from the moment the trip begins, it's obvious that something weird is going on. When they arrive, they find remnants of an awful blaze and a burned cabin. The campground's caretaker seems to be dead, but is he really gone?

INTERNET SITES

Do you want to know more about subjects related to this book? Or are you interested in learning about other topics? Then check out FactHound, a fun, easy way to find Internet sites.

Our investigative staff has already sniffed out great sites for you!

Here's how to use FactHound:

1. Visit *www.facthound.com*

2. Select your grade level.

3. To learn more about subjects related to this book, type in the book's ISBN number: **9781434207937**.

4. Click the **Fetch It** button.

FactHound will fetch the best Internet sites for you!